Fellow-Town

Fellow-Townsmen

Thomas Hardy

100 PAGES

Published by Hesperus Press Limited
4 Rickett Street, London SW6 1RU
www.hesperuspress.com

First published in 1880 in *New Quarterly Magazine*
First published by Hesperus Press Limited, 2003

Foreword © Emma Tennant, 2003

Designed and typeset by Fraser Muggeridge
Printed in the United Arab Emirates by Oriental Press

ISBN: 1-84391-038-1

CONTENTS

Foreword by Emma Tennant vii

Fellow-Townsmen 1
   Notes 73

Biographical note 75

FOREWORD

Accident or Destiny? The work of Thomas Hardy dwells obsessively on this question, whether in *Tess of the D'Urbervilles* where Fate ensured a dreadful trajectory for the poor heroine; or in poems where memories and missed opportunities, lost second chances, and an ill-disposed God rain down misfortune; or in short stories, especially in the gripping and yet somehow inevitable lot of Barnet and Lucy, the lovers of *Fellow-Townsmen*. 'Seize the day!' Hardy seems to be saying, as nineteenth-century constraints, wealth seeking and class consciousness occasion the fatal, faltering step. If you miss the first time, the punishment will be long and severe.

Thomas Hardy was forty years old when *Fellow-Townsmen* was published in April 1880, and the publication coincided with his decision to cease being a townsman himself. London was bad for his health, he concluded in that year of overwork and a probable pneumonia brought on by prolonged bathing off the coast of Normandy the summer before. He would return to Dorset, where his wife Emma – who was to prove a devoted nurse, even if considered mentally unstable once the efficient young Florence came on the scene – would ensure his well-being in the landscape he knew and loved best. And it's with Dorset that *Fellow-Townsmen* deals: Port Bredy, otherwise Bridport, and West Bay and Chesil Beach, much the same now as they were in the 1870s, provide the setting for a story where nothing remains the same at all, and Nature undoes good intentions and bad, alike. Those who try to win, we learn, are penalised more heavily even than the innocent victims of Destiny.

Barnet is a prosperous man; three generations of merchant-trading in the snug, grandly laid-out town of Bridport have enabled the building of a new house, high on the slopes of a green hill overlooking the town. We can just imagine the pretentious mid-nineteenth-century structure – the name 'Château Ringdale' on a placard outside the slowly rising pile – and we would be right to feel a certain derision for Mr Barnet. We have seen him in the company of an old Bridport friend, Downe, a struggling young lawyer, but blissfully happy in his marriage and family life, while Barnet is wedded to an aloof and snobbish lady whose past passion for Lord Ringdale has caused her to name the new house after him. Despicable Barnet, we are bound to think, as the two friends jog along to the less salubrious part of town where Downe's finances force him to live. Unlikeable Mr Barnet, with his inherited wealth, his loveless marriage and his idle existence! And sure enough, Destiny is just waiting to take the wretched Barnet and toss him up in the air.

The wonder of Thomas Hardy's talent is that he makes us care for this superfluous human being, in all his unknowingness of himself, and of the deeper meaning of the world. The first twinge of sympathy we experience, after Barnet's sickened realisation of his friend Downe's ecstatic matrimonial state, is when our hero visits a humble cottage down by the sea, where a former love of his life ekes out her existence by making decorative cards and living as frugally as Mr and Mrs Barnet consume expensively. With her Raphaelesque good looks, Lucy Savile is the prototypical Hardy heroine: punished early by the Fates for daring to exist at all, she lost a union with Barnet through a misunderstanding she was too humble and too unsure of herself to clear up. Now here he is – and he confesses the enduring love he feels for Lucy, and the failure of his marriage. Destiny, waiting up the chimney of the wind-battered abode on the shore, makes up for any missed opportunity here, and acts swiftly.

The story proceeds with the grim inevitability of the tides which come in on the pebbled beach and swirl into the tiny harbour. Mrs Downe, the kindly wife of the lawyer, invites Mrs Barnet to take a ride in a carriage, and then to go for a row on the placid waters of the bay. A storm gets up, the boat capsizes, and the figures of two lifeless women are brought ashore.

But here, the worldly concerns of Hardy the poet and romancer return to grip the story by the throat. For, just as Mrs Barnet, taken by her distraught husband up to their house, is pronounced dead by the local doctor, so do we remember that this doctor, Charlson by name, has passed Barnet in the street some time back and assured him he has every intention of repaying the fifty pounds he borrowed from the wealthy man within three weeks. What would the workings of Fate be, without money?

Now we understand that Barnet, with his wife dead – Mrs Downe's body is retrieved hours later: she is drowned, and no two ways about it – is suddenly in a position to marry his darling Lucy. Charlson, an unprincipled man with debts, has done Barnet an unexpectedly good turn.

Except for the fact that Mrs Barnet breathes, if very faintly. Had she been left, she would most certainly have died. But Barnet revives the wife for whom he feels neither affection nor concern. He becomes, though we may be reluctant to admit it, a kind of hero; he's a human being, at least, who refutes the doctor's terrible way of repaying what he owes.

A lifetime is encapsulated in *Fellow-Townsmen*, and the workings of the machine are grim. For, years later, when Mrs Barnet does die on a visit out of town, the news comes just too late for Barnet to act on it. And years later still, after an age wandering the face of the earth, when Barnet returns to his home town of Bridport, he finds Lucy widowed in turn. What will Destiny dictate for them? It is for the reader to discover, though it's fair to say that irony, another Hardy favourite, here comes into play.

– Emma Tennant, 2003

Fellow-Townsmen

CHAPTER ONE

The shepherd on the east hill could shout out lambing intelligence to the shepherd on the west hill, over the intervening town chimneys, without great inconvenience to his voice, so nearly did the steep pastures encroach upon the burghers' backyards. And at night it was possible to stand in the very midst of the town and hear from their native paddocks on the lower levels of greensward the mild lowing of the farmer's heifers, and the profound, warm blowings of breath in which those creatures indulge. But the community which had jammed itself in the valley thus flanked formed a veritable town, with a real mayor and corporation, and a staple manufacture.

During a certain damp evening five and thirty years ago, before the twilight was far advanced, a pedestrian of professional appearance, carrying a small bag in his hand and an elevated umbrella, was descending one of these hills by the turnpike road when he was overtaken by a phaeton.

'Hello, Downe – is that you?' said the driver of the vehicle, a young man of pale and refined appearance. 'Jump up here with me, and ride down to your door.'

The other turned a plump, cheery, rather self-indulgent face over his shoulder towards the hailer.

'Oh, good evening, Mr Barnet – thanks,' he said, and mounted beside his acquaintance.

They were fellow-burgesses of the town which lay beneath them, but though old and very good friends, they were differently circumstanced. Barnet was a richer man than the struggling young lawyer Downe, a fact which was to some extent perceptible in Downe's manner towards his companion, though nothing of it ever showed in Barnet's manner towards the solicitor. Barnet's position in the town was none of his own making; his father had been a very successful flax merchant in the same place, where the trade was still carried on as briskly as the small capacities of its quarters would allow. Having acquired a fair fortune, old Mr Barnet had retired from business, bringing up his son as a gentleman-burgher and, it must be added, as a well-educated, liberal-minded young man.

'How is Mrs Barnet?' asked Downe.

'Mrs Barnet was very well when I left home,' the other answered, constrainedly, exchanging his meditative regard of the horse for one of self-consciousness.

Mr Downe seemed to regret his enquiry, and immediately took up another thread of conversation. He congratulated his friend on his election as a councilman; he thought he had not seen him since that event took place; Mrs Downe had meant to call and congratulate Mrs Barnet, but he feared that she had failed to do so as yet.

Barnet seemed hampered in his replies. 'We should have been glad to see you. I – my wife would welcome Mrs Downe at any time, as you know… Yes, I am a member of the corporation – rather an inexperienced member, some of them say. It is quite true; and I should have declined the honour as premature – having other things on my hands just now, too – if it had not been pressed upon me so very heartily.'

'There is one thing you have on your hands which I can never quite see the necessity for,' said Downe, with good-humoured freedom. 'What the deuce do you want to build that new mansion for when you have already got such an excellent house as the one you live in?'

Barnet's face acquired a warmer shade of colour; but as the question had been idly asked by the solicitor while regarding the surrounding flocks and fields, he answered after a moment with no apparent embarrassment:

'Well, we wanted to get out of the town, you know: the house I am living in is rather old and inconvenient.'

Mr Downe declared that he had chosen a pretty site for the new building. They would be able to see for miles and miles from the windows. Was he going to give it a name? He supposed so.

Barnet thought not. There was no other house near that was likely to be mistaken for it. And he did not care for a name.

'But I think it has a name!' Downe observed. 'I went past – when was it? – this morning, and I saw something – "Château Ringdale", I think it was – stuck up on a board!'

'It was an idea she – we had for a short time,' said Barnet, hastily. 'But we have decided finally to do without a name – at any rate such a name as that. It must have been a week ago that you saw it. It was taken down last Saturday… Upon that matter I am firm!' he added, grimly.

Downe murmured in an unconvinced tone that he thought he had seen it yesterday.

Talking thus they drove into the town. The street was unusually still for the hour of seven in the evening; an increasing drizzle from the sea had prevailed since the afternoon, and now formed a gauze across the yellow lamps, and trickled with a gentle rattle down the heavy roofs of stone tile that bent the house-ridges hollow-backed with its weight, and in some instances caused the walls to bulge outwards in the upper storey. Their route took them past the little town hall, the Black Bull Hotel, and onward to the junction of a small street on the right, consisting of a row of those two-and-two windowed brick residences of no particular age which are exactly alike wherever found, except in the people they contain.

'Wait – I'll drive you up to your door,' said Barnet, when Downe prepared to alight at the corner. He thereupon turned into the narrow street, when the faces of three little girls could be discerned close to the panes of a lit window a few yards ahead, surmounted by that of a young matron, the gaze of all four being directed eagerly up the empty street. 'You are a fortunate fellow, Downe,' Barnet continued, as mother and children disappeared from the window to run to the door. 'You must be happy if any man is. I would give a hundred such houses as my new one to have a home like yours.'

'Well – yes, we get along pretty comfortably,' replied Downe, complacently.

'That house, Downe, is none of my ordering,' Barnet broke out, revealing a bitterness hitherto suppressed, and checking the horse a moment to finish his speech before delivering up his passenger. 'The house I have already is good enough for me, as you supposed. It is my own freehold; it was built by my grandfather, and is stout enough for a castle. My father was born there, lived there, and died there. I was born there, and have always lived there; yet I must needs build a new one.'

'Why do you?' said Downe.

'Why do I? To preserve peace in the household. I do anything for that; but I don't succeed. I was firm in resisting "Château Ringdale", however; not that I would not have put up with the absurdity of the name, but it was too much to have your house christened after Lord Ringdale because your wife once had a fancy for him. If you only knew everything, you would think all attempt at reconciliation hopeless. In your happy home you have had no such experiences, and God forbid that you ever should. See, here they are all ready to receive you!'

'Of course! And so will your wife be waiting to receive you,' said Downe. 'Take my word for it she will! And with a dinner prepared for you far better than mine.'

'I hope so,' Barnet replied, dubiously.

He moved on to Downe's door which the solicitor's family had already opened. Downe descended, but being encumbered with his bag and umbrella, his foot slipped, and he fell upon his knees in the gutter.

'Oh, my dear Charles!' said his wife, running down the steps; and, quite ignoring the presence of Barnet, she seized hold of her husband, pulled him to his feet, and kissed him, exclaiming, 'I hope you are not hurt, darling!' The children crowded round, chiming in piteously, 'Poor papa!'

'He's alright,' said Barnet, perceiving that Downe was only a little muddy, and looking more at the wife than at the husband. Almost at any other time – certainly during his fastidious bachelor years – he would have thought her a too demonstrative woman, but those recent circumstances of his own life to which he had just alluded made Mrs Downe's solicitude so affecting that his eye grew damp as he witnessed it. Bidding the lawyer and his family goodnight, he left them, and drove slowly into the main street towards his own house.

The heart of Barnet was sufficiently impressionable to be influenced by Downe's parting prophecy that he might not be so unwelcome home as he imagined: the dreary night might, at least on this one occasion, make Downe's forecast true. Hence it was in a suspense that he could hardly have believed possible that he halted at his door. On entering, his wife was nowhere to be seen, and he enquired for her. The servant informed him that her mistress had the dressmaker with her, and would be engaged for some time.

'Dressmaker at this time of day!'

'She dined early, sir, and hopes you will excuse her joining you this evening.'

'But she knew I was coming tonight?'

'Oh yes, sir.'

'Go up and tell her I am come.'

The servant did so, but the mistress of the house merely transmitted her former words.

Barnet said nothing more, and presently sat down to his lonely meal, which was eaten abstractedly, the domestic scene he had lately witnessed still impressing him by its contrast with the situation here. His mind fell back into past years upon a certain pleasing and gentle being whose face would loom out of their shades at such times as these. Barnet turned in his chair, and looked with unfocused eyes in a direction southward from where he sat, as if he saw not the room but a long way beyond. 'I wonder if she lives there still?' he said.

CHAPTER TWO

He rose with a sudden rebelliousness, put on his hat and coat, and went out of the house, pursuing his way along the glistening pavement while eight o'clock was striking from St Mary's tower, and the apprentices and shopmen were slamming up the shutters from end to end of the town. In two minutes, only those shops which could boast of no attendant save the master or the mistress remained with open eyes. These were ever somewhat less prompt to exclude customers than the others: for their owners' ears the closing hour had scarcely the cheerfulness that it possessed for the hired servants of the rest. Yet the night being dreary the delay was not for long, and their windows, too, blinked together one by one.

During this time Barnet had proceeded with decided step in a direction at right angles to the broad main thoroughfare of the town, by a long street leading due southward. Here, though his family had no more to do with the flax manufacture, his own name occasionally greeted him on gates and warehouses, being used allusively by small rising tradesmen as a recommendation, in such words as 'Smith, from Barnet & Co.', 'Robinson, late manager at Barnet's'. The sight led him to reflect upon his father's busy life, and he questioned if it had not been far happier than his own.

The houses along the road became fewer, and presently open ground appeared between them on either side, the track on the right hand rising to a higher level till it merged in a knoll. On the summit a row of builders' scaffold poles probed the indistinct sky like spears, and at their bases could be discerned the lower courses of a building lately begun. Barnet slackened his pace and stood for a few moments without leaving the centre of the road, apparently not much interested in the sight, till suddenly his eye was caught by a post in the forepart of the ground bearing a white board at the top. He went to the rails, vaulted over, and walked in far enough to discern painted upon the board 'Château Ringdale'.

A dismal irony seemed to lie in the words, and its effect was to irritate him. Downe, then, had spoken truly. He stuck his umbrella into the sod, and seized the post with both hands, as if intending to loosen and throw it down. Then, like one bewildered by an opposition which would exist none the less though its manifestations were removed, he allowed his arms to sink to his side.

'Let it be,' he said to himself. 'I have declared there shall be peace – if possible.'

Taking up his umbrella he quietly left the enclosure, and went on his way, still keeping his back to the town. He had advanced with more decision since passing the new building, and soon a hoarse murmur rose upon the gloom; it was the sound of the sea. The road led to the harbour, at a distance of a mile from the town, from which the trade of the district was fed. After seeing the obnoxious name-board Barnet had forgotten to open his umbrella, and the rain tapped smartly on his hat, and occasionally stroked his face as he went on.

Though the lamps were still continued at the roadside, they stood at wider intervals than before, and the pavement had given place to common road. Every time he came to a lamp, an increasing shine made itself visible upon his shoulders till at last they quite glistened with wet. The murmur from the shore grew stronger, but it was still some distance off when he paused before one of the smallest of the detached houses by the wayside, standing in its own garden, the latter being divided from the road by a row of wooden palings. Scrutinising the spot to ensure that he was not mistaken, he opened the gate and gently knocked at the cottage door.

When he had patiently waited minutes enough to lead any man in ordinary cases to knock again, the door was heard to open, though it was impossible to see by whose hand, there being no light in the passage. Barnet said at random, 'Does Miss Savile live here?'

A youthful voice assured him that she did live there, and by a sudden afterthought asked him to come in. It would soon get a light, it said: but the night being wet, mother had not thought it worthwhile to trim the passage lamp.

'Don't trouble yourself to get a light for me,' said Barnet, hastily. 'It is not necessary at all. Which is Miss Savile's sitting-room?'

The young person, whose white pinafore could just be discerned, signified a door in the side of the passage, and Barnet went forward at the same moment, so that no light should fall upon his face. On entering the room he closed the door behind him, pausing till he heard the retreating footsteps of the child.

He found himself in an apartment which was simply and neatly, though not poorly, furnished; everything, from the miniature chiffonnier to the shining little daguerreotype which formed the central ornament of the mantelpiece, being in scrupulous order. The picture was enclosed by a frame of embroidered cardboard – evidently the work of feminine hands – and it was the portrait of a thin-faced, elderly lieutenant in the navy. From behind the lamp on the table a female form now rose into view, that of a young girl, and a resemblance between her and the portrait was early discoverable. She had been so absorbed in some occupation on the other side of the lamp as to have barely found time to realise her visitor's presence.

They both remained standing for a few seconds without speaking. The face that confronted Barnet had a beautiful outline – the Raphaelesque oval of its contour was remarkable for an English countenance, and that countenance housed in a remote country road to an unheard-of harbour. But her features did not do justice to this splendid beginning: Nature had recollected that she was not in Italy; and the young lady's lineaments, though not so inconsistent as to make her plain, would have been accepted rather as pleasing than as correct. The preoccupied expression which, like images on the retina, remained with her for a moment after the state that caused it had ceased, now changed into a reserved, half-proud, and slightly indignant look in which the blood diffused itself quickly across her cheek, and additional brightness broke the shade of her rather heavy eyes.

'I know I have no business here,' he said, answering the look. 'But I had a great wish to see you, and enquire how you were. You can give your hand to me, seeing how often I have held it in past days?'

'I would rather forget than remember all that, Mr Barnet,' she answered, as she coldly complied with the request. 'When I think of the circumstances of our last meeting, I can hardly consider it kind of you to allude to such a thing as our past – or, indeed, to come here at all.'

'There was no harm in it surely? I don't trouble you often, Lucy.'

'I have not had the honour of a visit from you for a very long time, certainly, and I did not expect it now,' she said, with the same stiffness in her air. 'I hope Mrs Barnet is very well?'

'Yes, yes!' he impatiently returned. 'At least I suppose so – though I only speak from inference!'

'But she is your wife, sir,' said the young girl, tremulously.

The unwonted tones of a man's voice in that feminine chamber had startled a canary that was roosting in its cage by the window; the bird awoke hastily, and fluttered against the bars. She went and stilled it by laying her face against the cage and murmuring a coaxing sound. It might partly have been done to still herself.

'I didn't come to talk of Mrs Barnet,' he pursued; 'I came to talk of you, of yourself alone; to enquire how you are getting on since your great loss.' And he turned towards the portrait of her father.

'I am getting on fairly well, thank you.'

The force of her utterance was scarcely borne out by her look, but Barnet courteously reproached himself for not having guessed a thing so natural; and to dissipate all embarrassment added, as he bent over the table, 'What were you doing when I came? – painting flowers, and by candlelight?'

'Oh no,' she said, 'not painting them – only sketching

13

the outlines. I do that at night to save time – I have to get three dozen done by the end of the month.'

Barnet looked as if he regretted it deeply. 'You will wear your poor eyes out,' he said, with more sentiment than he had hitherto shown. 'You ought not to do it. There was a time when I should have said you must not. Well – I almost wish I had never seen light with my own eyes when I think of that!'

'Is this a time or place for recalling such matters?' she asked, with dignity. 'You used to have a gentlemanly respect for me, and for yourself. Don't speak any more as you have spoken, and don't come again. I cannot think that this visit is serious, or was closely considered by you.'

'Considered: well, I came to see you as an old and good friend – not to mince matters, to visit a woman I loved. Don't be angry! I could not help doing it, so many things brought you into my mind… This evening I fell in with an acquaintance, and when I saw how happy he was with his wife and family welcoming him home, though with only one-tenth of my income and chances, and thought what might have been in my case, it fairly broke down my discretion, and off I came here. Now I am here I feel that I am wrong to some extent. But the feeling that I should like to see you, and talk of those we used to know in common, was very strong.'

'Before that can be the case a little more time must pass,' said Miss Savile, quietly; 'a time long enough for me to regard with some calmness what at present I remember far too impatiently – though it may be you almost forget it. Indeed you must have forgotten it long before you acted as you did.' Her voice grew stronger and more vivacious as she added: 'But I am doing my best to forget it too, and I know I shall succeed from the progress I have made already!'

She had remained standing till now, when she turned and sat down, facing half away from him.

Barnet watched her moodily. 'Yes, it is only what I deserve,' he said. 'Ambition pricked me on – no, it was not ambition, it was wrong-headedness! Had I but reflected…'

He broke out vehemently: 'But always remember this, Lucy: if you had written to me only one little line after that misunderstanding, I declare I should have come back to you. That ruined me!' He slowly walked as far as the little room would allow him to go, and remained with his eyes on the skirting.

'But, Mr Barnet, how could I write to you? There was no opening for my doing so.'

'Then there ought to have been,' said Barnet, turning. 'That was my fault!'

'Well, I don't know anything about that; but as there had been nothing said by me which required any explanation by letter, I did not send one. Everything was so indefinite, and feeling your position to be so much wealthier than mine, I fancied I might have mistaken your meaning. And when I heard of the other lady – a woman of whose family even you might be proud – I thought how foolish I had been, and said nothing.'

'Then I suppose it was destiny – accident – I don't know what, that separated us, dear Lucy. Anyhow you were the woman I ought to have made my wife – and I let you slip, like the foolish man that I was!'

'Oh, Mr Barnet,' she said, almost in tears, 'don't revive the subject to me; I am the wrong one to console you – think, sir – you should not be here – it would be so bad for me if it were known!'

'It would – it would, indeed,' he said, hastily. 'I am not right in doing this, and I won't do it again.'

'It is a very common folly of human nature, you know, to think the course you did *not* adopt must have been the best,' she continued, with gentle solicitude, as she followed him to the door of the room. 'And you don't know that I should have accepted you, even if you had asked me to be your wife.' At this his eye met hers, and she dropped her gaze. She knew that her voice belied her. There was a silence till she looked up to add, in a voice of soothing playfulness, 'My family was so much poorer than yours, even before I lost my dear father, that… perhaps your companions would have made it unpleasant for us on account of my deficiencies.'

'Your disposition would soon have won them round,' said Barnet.

She archly expostulated: 'Now, never mind my disposition; try to make it up with your wife! Those are my commands to you. And now you are to leave me at once.'

'I will. I must make the best of it all, I suppose,' he replied, more cheerfully than he had as yet spoken. 'But I shall never again meet with such a dear girl as you!' And he suddenly opened the door, and left her alone. When his glance again fell on the lamps that were sparsely ranged along the dreary level road, his eyes were in a state which showed straw-like motes of light radiating from each flame into the surrounding air.

On the other side of the way Barnet observed a man under an umbrella, walking parallel with himself. Presently this man left the footway, and gradually converged on Barnet's course. The latter then saw that it was Charlson, a surgeon of the town, who owed him money.

Charlson was a man not without ability; yet he did not prosper. Sundry circumstances stood in his way as a medical practitioner: he was needy; he was not a coddle; he gossiped with men instead of with women; he had married a stranger instead of one of the town young ladies; and he was given to conversational buffoonery. Moreover, his look was quite erroneous. Those only proper features in the family doctor – the quiet eye, and the thin straight passionless lips which never curl in public either for laughter or for scorn – were not his; he had a full-curved mouth, and a bold black eye that made timid people nervous. His companions were what in old times would have been called boon companions – an expression which, though of irreproachable root, suggests fraternisation carried to the point of unscrupulousness. All this was against him in the little town of his adoption.

Charlson had been in difficulties, and to oblige him Barnet had put his name to a bill; and, as he had expected, was called upon to meet it when it fell due. It had been only a matter of fifty pounds, which Barnet could well afford to lose, and he bore no ill will to the thriftless surgeon on account of it. But Charlson had a little too much brazen indifferentism in his composition to be altogether a desirable acquaintance.

'I hope to be able to make that little bill business right with you in the course of three weeks, Mr Barnet,' said Charlson, with hail-fellow friendliness.

Barnet replied good-naturedly that there was no hurry.

This particular three weeks had moved on in advance of Charlson's present with the precision of a shadow for some considerable time.

'I've had a dream,' Charlson continued. Barnet knew from his tone that the surgeon was going to begin his characteristic nonsense, and did not encourage him. 'I've had a dream,' repeated Charlson, who required no encouragement. 'I dreamt that a gentleman, who has been very kind to me, married a haughty lady in haste, before he had quite forgotten a nice little girl he knew before, and that one wet evening, like the present, as I was walking up the harbour road, I saw him come out of that dear little girl's present abode.'

Barnet glanced towards the speaker. The rays from a neighbouring lamp struck through the drizzle under Charlson's umbrella so as just to illumine his face against the shade behind, and show that his eye was turned up under the outer corner of its lid, whence it leered with impish jocoseness as he thrust his tongue into his cheek.

'Come,' said Barnet, gravely, 'we'll have no more of that.'

'No, no – of course not,' Charlson hastily answered, seeing that his humour had carried him too far, as it had done many times before. He was profuse in his apologies, but Barnet did not reply. Of one thing he was certain – that scandal was a plant of quick root, and that he was bound to obey Lucy's injunction for Lucy's own sake.

CHAPTER THREE

He did so, to the letter; and though, as the crocus followed the snowdrop and the daffodil the crocus in Lucy's garden, the harbour road was a not unpleasant place to walk in, Barnet's feet never trod its stones, much less approached her door. He avoided a saunter that way as he would have avoided a dangerous dram, and took his airings a long distance northward, among severely square and brown ploughed fields, where no other townsman came. Sometimes he went round by the lower lanes of the borough, where the rope-walks stretched in which his family formerly had share, and looked at the rope-makers walking backwards, overhung by apple trees and bushes, and intruded on by cows and calves, as if trade had established itself there at considerable inconvenience to Nature.

One morning, when the sun was so warm as to raise a steam from the south-eastern slopes of those flanking hills that looked so lovely above the old roofs, but made every low-chimneyed house in the town as smoky as Tophet[1], Barnet glanced from the windows of the town-council room for lack of interest in what was proceeding within. Several members of the corporation were present, but there was not much business doing, and in a few minutes Downe came leisurely across to him, saying that he seldom saw Barnet now.

Barnet owned that he was not often present.

Downe looked at the crimson curtain which hung down beside the panes, reflecting its hot hues into their faces, and then out of the window. At that moment there passed along the street a tall commanding lady, in whom the solicitor recognised Barnet's wife. Barnet had done the same thing, and turned away.

'It will be alright some day,' said Downe, with cheering sympathy.

'You have heard, then, of her last outbreak?'

Downe depressed his cheerfulness to its very reverse in a moment. 'No, I have not heard of anything serious,' he said, with as long a face as one naturally round could be turned into at short notice. 'I only hear vague reports of such things.'

'You may think it will be alright,' said Barnet, drily. 'But I have a different opinion… No, Downe, we must look the thing in the face. Not poppy, nor mandragora – however, how are your wife and children?'

Downe said that they were all well, thanks; they were out that morning somewhere; he was just looking to see if they were walking that way. Ah, there they were, just coming down the street; and Downe pointed to the figures of two children with a nursemaid, and a lady walking behind them.

'You will come out and speak to her?' he asked.

'Not this morning. The fact is I don't care to speak to anybody just now.'

'You are too sensitive, Mr Barnet. At school I remember you used to get as red as a rose if anybody uttered a word that hurt your feelings.'

Barnet mused. 'Yes,' he admitted, 'there is a grain of truth in that. It is because of that I often try to make peace at home. Life would be tolerable then at any rate, even if not particularly bright.'

'I have thought more than once of proposing a little plan to you,' said Downe, with some hesitation. 'I don't know whether it will meet your views, but take it or leave it, as you choose. In fact, it was my wife who suggested it: that she would be very glad to call on Mrs Barnet and get into her confidence. She seems to think that Mrs Barnet is rather alone in the town, and without advisers. Her impression is that your wife will listen to reason. Emily has a wonderful way of winning the hearts of people of her own sex.'

'And of the other sex too, I think. She is a charming woman, and you were a lucky fellow to find her.'

'Well, perhaps I was,' simpered Downe, trying to wear an aspect of being the last man in the world to feel pride. 'However, she will be likely to find out what ruffles Mrs Barnet. Perhaps it is some misunderstanding, you know – something that she is too proud to ask you to explain, or some little thing in your conduct that irritates her because she does not fully comprehend you. The truth is, Emily would have been more ready to make advances if she had been quite sure of her fitness for Mrs Barnet's society, who has of course been accustomed to London people of good position, which made Emily fearful of intruding.'

Barnet expressed his warmest thanks for the well-intentioned proposition. There was reason in Mrs Downe's fear – that he owned. 'But do let her call,' he said. 'There is no woman in England I would so soon trust on such an errand. I am afraid there will not be any brilliant result; still I shall take it as the kindest and nicest thing if she will try it, and not be frightened at a repulse.'

When Barnet and Downe had parted, the former went

to the Town Savings Bank, of which he was a trustee, and endeavoured to forget his troubles in the contemplation of low sums of money and figures in a network of red and blue lines. He sat and watched the working people making their deposits, to which at intervals he signed his name. Before he left in the afternoon Downe put his head inside the door.

'Emily has seen Mrs Barnet,' he said, in a low voice. 'She has got Mrs Barnet's promise to take her for a drive down to the shore tomorrow, if it is fine. Good afternoon!'

Barnet shook Downe by the hand without speaking, and Downe went away.

CHAPTER FOUR

The next day was as fine as the arrangement could possibly require. As the sun passed the meridian and declined westward, the tall shadows from the scaffold poles of Barnet's rising residence streaked the ground as far as to the middle of the highway. Barnet himself was there inspecting the progress of the works for the first time during several weeks. A building in an old-fashioned town five and thirty years ago did not, as in the modern fashion, rise from the sod like a booth at a fair. The foundations and lower courses were put in and allowed to settle for many weeks before the superstructure was built up, and a whole summer of drying was hardly sufficient to do justice to the important issues involved. Barnet stood within a window-niche which had as yet received no frame, and thence looked down a slope into the road. The wheels of a chaise were heard, and then his handsome Xanthippe[2], in the company of Mrs Downe, drove past on their way to the shore. They were driving slowly; there was a pleasing light in Mrs Downe's face which seemed faintly to reflect itself upon the countenance of her companion – that *politesse du coeur* which was so natural to her having possibly begun already to work results. But whatever the situation, Barnet resolved not to interfere, or do anything to hazard the promise of the day. He might well afford to trust the issue to another when he could never direct it but to ill himself. His wife's clenched rein-hand in its lemon-coloured glove, her stiff erect figure, clad in velvet and lace, and her boldly outlined face, passed on, exhibiting their owner as one fixed for ever above the level of her companion – socially by her early breeding, and materially by her higher cushion.

Barnet decided to allow them a proper time to themselves, and then stroll down to the shore and drive them home. After lingering on at the house for another hour he started with this intention. A few hundred yards below Château Ringdale stood the cottage in which the late lieutenant's daughter had her lodging. Barnet had not been so far that way for a long time, and as he approached the forbidden ground a curious warmth passed into him, which led him to perceive that, unless he were careful, he might have to fight the battle with himself about Lucy over again. A tenth of his present excuse would, however, have justified him in travelling by that road today.

He came opposite the dwelling, and turned his eyes for a momentary glance into the little garden that stretched from the palings to the door. Lucy was in the enclosure; she was walking and stooping to gather some flowers, possibly for the purpose of painting them, for she moved about quickly, as if anxious to save time. She did not see him; he might have passed unnoticed, but a sensation which was not in strict unison with his previous sentiments that day led him to pause in his walk and watch her. She went nimbly round and round the beds of anemones, tulips, jonquils, polyanthuses, and other old-fashioned flowers, looking a very charming figure in her half-mourning bonnet, and with an incomplete nosegay in her left hand. Raising herself to pull down a lilac blossom, she observed him.

'Mr Barnet!' she said, innocently smiling. 'Why, I have been thinking of you many times since Mrs Barnet went by in the pony-carriage, and now here you are!'

'Yes, Lucy,' he said.

Then she seemed to recall particulars of their last meeting, and he believed that she flushed, though it might have been only the fancy of his own supersensitiveness.

'I am going to the harbour,' he added.

'Are you?' Lucy remarked, simply. 'A great many people begin to go there now the summer is drawing on.'

Her face had come more into his view as she spoke, and he noticed how much thinner and paler it was than when he had seen it last. 'Lucy, how weary you look! Tell me, can I help you?' he was going to cry out. '– If I do,' he thought, 'it will be the ruin of us both!' He merely said that the afternoon was fine, and went on his way.

As he went a sudden blast of air came over the hill as if in contradiction to his words, and spoilt the previous quiet of the scene. The wind had already shifted violently, and now smelt of the sea.

The harbour road soon began to justify its name. A gap appeared in the rampart of hills which shut out the sea, and on the left of the opening rose a vertical cliff, coloured a burning orange by the sunlight, the companion cliff on the right being livid in shade. Between these cliffs, like the Libyan bay which sheltered the shipwrecked Trojans[3], was a little haven, seemingly a beginning made by Nature herself of a perfect harbour, which appealed to the passer-by as only requiring a little human industry to finish it and make it famous, the ground on each side as far back as the daisied slopes that bounded the interior valley being a mere layer of blown sand. But the Port Bredy burgesses a mile inland had, in the course of ten centuries, responded many times to that mute appeal, with the result that the tides had invariably choked up their works with sand and shingle as soon as completed. There were but few houses here: a rough pier, a few boats, some stores, an inn, a residence or two, a ketch unloading in the harbour, were the chief features of the settlement. On the open ground by the shore stood his wife's pony-carriage, empty, the boy in attendance holding the horse.

When Barnet drew nearer, he saw an indigo-coloured spot moving swiftly along beneath the radiant base of the eastern cliff, which proved to be a man in a jersey, running with all his might. He held up his hand to Barnet, as it seemed, and they approached each other. The man was local, but a stranger to him.

'What is it, my man?' said Barnet.

'A terrible calamity!' the boatman hastily explained. Two ladies had been capsized in a boat – they were Mrs Downe and Mrs Barnet of the old town; they had driven down there that afternoon – they had alighted, and it was so fine that, after walking about a little while, they had been tempted to go out for a short sail round the cliff. Just as they were putting in to the shore, the wind shifted with a sudden gust, the boat listed over, and it was thought they were both drowned. How it could have happened was beyond his mind to fathom, for John Green knew how to sail a boat as well as any man there.

'Which is the way to the place?' said Barnet.

It was just round the cliff.

'Run to the carriage and tell the boy to bring it to the place as soon as you can. Then go to the Harbour Inn and tell them to ride to town for a doctor. Have they been got out of the water?'

'One lady has.'

'Which?'

'Mrs Barnet. Mrs Downe, it is feared, has fleeted out to sea.'

Barnet ran on to that part of the shore which the cliff had hitherto obscured from his view, and there discerned, a long way ahead, a group of fishermen standing. As soon as he came up one or two recognised him, and, not liking to meet his eye, turned aside with misgiving. He went amidst them and saw a small sailing boat lying draggled at the water's edge; and, on the sloping shingle beside it, a soaked and sandy woman's form in the velvet dress and yellow gloves of his wife.

CHAPTER FIVE

All had been done that could be done. Mrs Barnet was in her own house under medical hands, but the result was still uncertain. Barnet had acted as if devotion to his wife were the dominant passion of his existence. There had been much to decide: whether to attempt restoration of the apparently lifeless body as it lay on the shore; whether to carry her to the Harbour Inn; whether to drive with her at once to his own house. The first course, with no skilled help or appliances near at hand, had seemed hopeless. The second course would have occupied nearly as much time as a drive to the town owing to the intervening ridges of shingle, and the necessity of crossing the harbour by boat to get to the house, added to which much time must have elapsed before a doctor could have arrived down there. By bringing her home in the carriage some precious moments had slipped by; but she had been laid in her own bed in seven minutes, a doctor called to her side, and every possible restorative brought to bear upon her.

At what a tearing pace he had driven up that road, through the yellow evening sunlight, the shadows flapping irksomely into his eyes as each wayside object rushed past between him and the west! Tired workmen with their baskets at their backs had turned on their homeward journey to wonder at his speed. Halfway between the shore and Port Bredy town he had met Charlson who had been the first surgeon to hear of the accident. He was accompanied by his assistant in a gig. Barnet had sent on the latter to the coast in case that Downe's poor wife should by that time have been reclaimed from the waves, and had brought Charlson back with him to the house.

Barnet's presence was not needed here, and he felt it to be his next duty to set off at once and find Downe, that no other than himself might break the news to him.

He was quite sure that no chance had been lost for Mrs Downe by his leaving the shore. By the time that Mrs Barnet had been laid in the carriage, a much larger group had assembled to lend assistance in finding her friend, rendering his own help superfluous. But the duty of breaking the news was made doubly painful by the circumstance that the catastrophe which had befallen Mrs Downe was solely the result of her own and her husband's loving-kindness towards himself.

He found Downe in his office. When the solicitor comprehended the intelligence he turned pale, stood up, and remained for a moment perfectly still, as if bereft of his faculties; then his shoulders heaved, he pulled out his handkerchief and began to cry like a child. His sobs might have been heard in the next room. He seemed to have no idea of going to the shore, or of doing anything; but when Barnet took him gently by the hand and proposed to start at once, he quietly acquiesced, neither uttering any further word nor making any effort to repress his tears.

Barnet accompanied him to the shore, where, finding that no trace had as yet been seen of Mrs Downe, and that his stay would be of no avail, he left Downe with his friends and the young doctor, and once more hastened back to his own house.

At the door he met Charlson. 'Well?' Barnet said.

'I have just come down,' said the doctor. 'We have done

everything, but without result. I sympathise with you in your bereavement.'

Barnet did not much appreciate Charlson's sympathy, which sounded to his ears as something of a mockery from the lips of a man who knew what Charlson knew about their domestic relations. Indeed there seemed an odd spark in Charlson's full black eye as he said the words; but that might have been imaginary.

'And, Mr Barnet,' Charlson resumed, 'that little matter between us – I hope to settle it finally in three weeks at least.'

'Never mind that now,' said Barnet, abruptly. He directed the surgeon to go to the harbour in case his services might even now be necessary there, and himself entered the house.

The servants were coming from his wife's chamber, looking helplessly at each other and at him. He passed them by and entered the room, where he stood regarding the shape on the bed for a few minutes, after which he walked into his own dressing-room adjoining, and there paced up and down. In a minute or two he noticed what a strange and total silence had come over the upper part of the house; his own movements, muffled as they were by the carpet, seemed noisy, and his thoughts to disturb the air like articulate utterances. His eye glanced through the window. Far down the road to the harbour a roof detained his gaze: out of it rose a red chimney, and out of the red chimney a curl of smoke, as from a fire newly kindled. He had often seen such a sight before. In that house lived Lucy Savile, and the smoke was from the fire which was regularly lit at this time to make her tea.

After that he went back to the bedroom, and stood there some time regarding his wife's silent form. She was a woman some years older than himself, but had not by any means overpassed the maturity of good looks and vigour. Her passionate features, well-defined, firm, and statuesque in life, were doubly so now: her mouth and brow, beneath her purplish black hair, showed only too clearly that the turbulency of character which had made a beargarden of his house had been no temporary phase of her existence. While he reflected, he suddenly said to himself: 'I wonder if all has been done?'

The thought was led up to by his having fancied that his wife's features lacked in its completeness the expression which he had been accustomed to associate with the faces of those whose spirits have fled for ever. The effacement of life was not so marked but that, entering uninformed, he might have supposed her sleeping. Her complexion was that seen in the numerous faded portraits by Sir Joshua Reynolds; it was pallid in comparison with life, but there was visible on a close inspection the remnant of what had once been a flush; the keeping between the cheeks and the hollows of the face being thus preserved, although positive colour was gone. Long orange rays of evening sun stole in through chinks in the blind, striking on the large mirror, and being thence reflected upon the crimson hangings and woodwork of the heavy bedstead, so that the general tone of light was remarkably warm; and it was probable that something might be due to this circumstance. Still the fact impressed him as strange. Charlson had been gone more than a quarter of an hour: could it be possible that he had left too soon, and that his attempts to restore her had operated so sluggishly as only now to have made themselves felt? Barnet laid his hand upon her chest, and fancied that ever and anon a faint flutter of palpitation, gentle as that of a butterfly's wing, disturbed the stillness there – ceasing for a time, then struggling to go on, then breaking down in weakness and ceasing again.

Barnet's mother had been an active practitioner of the healing art among her poorer neighbours, and her inspirations had all been derived from an octavo volume of *Domestic Medicine*, which at this moment was lying, as it had lain for many years, on a shelf in Barnet's dressing-room. He hastily fetched it, and there read under the head 'Drowning':

> *Exertions for the recovery of any person who has not been immersed for a longer period than half an hour should be continued for at least four hours, as there have been many cases in which returning life has made itself visible even after a longer interval.*
>
> *Should, however, a weak action of any of the organs show itself when the case seems almost hopeless, our efforts must be redoubled; the feeble spark in this case requires to be solicited; it will certainly disappear under a relaxation of labour.*

Barnet looked at his watch; it was now barely two hours and a half from the time when he had first heard of the accident. He threw aside the book, and turned quickly to reach a stimulant which had previously been used. Pulling up the blind for more light, his eye glanced out of the window. There he saw that red chimney still smoking cheerily, and that roof, and through the roof that some-body. His mechanical movements stopped, his hand remained on the blind-cord, and he seemed to become breathless, as if he had suddenly found himself treading a high rope.

While he stood a sparrow lighted on the window-sill, saw him, and flew away. Next a man and a dog walked over one of the green hills which bulged above the roofs of the town. But Barnet took no notice.

We may wonder what were the exact images that passed through his mind during those minutes of gazing upon Lucy Savile's house, the sparrow, the man and the dog, and Lucy Savile's house again. There are honest men who will not admit to their thoughts, even as idle hypotheses, views of the future that assume as done a deed which they would recoil from doing; and there are other honest men for whom morality ends at the surface of their own heads, who will deliberate what the first will not so much as suppose. Barnet had a wife whose presence distracted his home; she now lay as in death. By merely doing nothing – by letting the intelligence which had gone forth to the world lie undisturbed – he would effect such a deliverance for himself as he had never hoped for, and open up an opportunity of which till now he had never dreamt. Whether the conjuncture had arisen through any unscrupulous, ill-considered impulse of Charlson to help out of a strait the friend who was so kind as never to press him for what was due could not be told; there was nothing to prove it, and it was a question which could never be asked. The triangular situation – himself – his wife – Lucy Savile – was the one clear thing.

From Barnet's actions we may infer that he *supposed* such and such a result for a moment, but did not deliberate. He withdrew his hazel eyes from the scene without, calmly turned, rang the bell for assistance, and vigorously exerted himself to learn if life still lingered in that motionless frame. In a short time another surgeon was in attendance; and then Barnet's surmise proved to be true. The slow life timidly heaved again; but much care and patience were needed to catch and retain it, and a considerable period elapsed before it could be said with certainty that Mrs Barnet lived. When this was the case, and there was no further room for doubt, Barnet left the chamber. The blue evening smoke from Lucy's chimney had died down to an imperceptible stream, and as he walked about downstairs he murmured to himself, 'My wife was dead, and she is alive again.'

It was not so with Downe. After three hours' immersion his wife's body had been recovered – life, of course, being quite extinct. Barnet, on descending, went straight to his friend's house, and there learnt the result. Downe was helpless in his wild grief, occasionally even hysterical. Barnet said little, but finding that some guiding hand was necessary in the sorrow-stricken household, took upon him to supervise and manage till Downe should be in a state of mind to do so for himself.

CHAPTER SIX

One September evening, four months later, when Mrs Barnet was in perfect health, and Mrs Downe but a weakening memory, an errand-boy paused to rest himself in front of Mr Barnet's old house, depositing his basket on one of the window-sills. The street was not yet lit, but there were lights in the house, and at intervals a flitting shadow fell upon the blind at his elbow. Words also were audible from the same apartment, and they seemed to be those of persons in violent altercation. But the boy could not gather their purport, and he went on his way.

Ten minutes afterwards the door of Barnet's house opened, and a tall closely veiled lady in a travelling dress came out and descended the freestone steps. The servant stood in the doorway watching her as she went with a measured tread down the street. When she had been out of sight for some minutes Barnet appeared at the door from within.

'Did your mistress leave word where she was going?' he asked.

'No, sir.'

'Is the carriage ordered to meet her anywhere?'

'No, sir.'

'Did she take a latchkey?'

'No, sir.'

Barnet went in again, sat down in his chair, and leant back. Then in solitude and silence he brooded over the bitter emotions that filled his heart. It was for this that he had gratuitously restored her to life and made his union with another impossible! The evening drew on, and nobody came to disturb him. At bedtime he told the servants to retire, that he would sit up for Mrs Barnet himself; and when they were gone he leant his head upon his hand and mused for hours.

The clock struck one, two; still his wife came not, and, with impatience added to depression, he went from room to room till another weary hour had passed. This was not altogether a new experience for Barnet; but she had never before so prolonged her absence. At last he sat down again and fell asleep.

He awoke at six o'clock to find that she had not returned. In searching about the rooms he discovered that she had taken a case of jewels which had been hers before her marriage. At eight a note was brought him; it was from his wife, in which she stated that she had gone by the coach to the house of a distant relative near London, and expressed a wish that certain boxes, articles of clothing, and so on, might be sent to her forthwith. The note was brought to him by a waiter at the Black Bull Hotel, and had been written by Mrs Barnet immediately before she took her place in the stage.

By the evening this order was carried out, and Barnet, with a sense of relief, walked out into the town. A fair had been held during the day, and the large clear moon which rose over the most prominent hill flung its light upon the booths and standings that still remained in the street, mixing its rays curiously with those from the flaring naphtha lamps. The town was full of country-people who had come in to enjoy themselves, and on this account Barnet strolled through the streets unobserved. With a certain recklessness he made for the harbour road, and presently found himself by the shore, where he walked on till he came to the spot near which his friend, the kindly Mrs Downe, had lost her life, and his own wife's life had been preserved. A tremulous pathway of bright moonshine now stretched over the water which had engulfed them, and not a living soul was near.

Here he ruminated on their characters, and next on the young girl in whom he now took a more sensitive interest than at the time when he had been free to marry her. Nothing, so far as he was aware, had ever appeared in his own conduct to show that such an interest existed. He had made it a point of the utmost strictness to hinder that feeling from influencing in the faintest degree his attitude towards his wife; and this was made all the more easy for him by the small demand Mrs Barnet made upon his attentions, for which she ever evinced the greatest contempt; thus unwittingly giving him the satisfaction of knowing that their severance owed nothing to jealousy, or, indeed, to any personal behaviour of his at all. Her concern was not with him or his feelings, as she frequently told him; but that she had, in a moment of weakness, thrown herself away upon a common burgher when she might have aimed at, and possibly brought down, a peer of the realm. Her frequent depreciation of Barnet in these terms had at times been so intense that he was sorely tempted to retaliate on her egotism by owning that he loved at the same low level on which he lived; but prudence had prevailed, for which he was now thankful.

Something seemed to sound upon the shingle behind him over and above the raking of the wave. He looked round, and a slight girlish shape appeared quite close to him. He could not see her face because it was in the direction of the moon.

'Mr Barnet?' the rambler said, in timid surprise. The voice was the voice of Lucy Savile.

'Yes,' said Barnet. 'How can I repay you for this pleasure?'

'I only came because the night was so clear. I am now on my way home.'

'I am glad we have met. I want to know if you will let me do something for you, to give me an occupation, as an idle man? I am sure I ought to help you, for I know you are almost without friends.'

She hesitated. 'Why should you tell me that?' she said.

'In the hope that you will be frank with me.'

'I am not altogether without friends here. But I am going to make a little change in my life – to go out as a teacher of free-hand drawing and practical perspective, of course I mean on a comparatively humble scale, because I have not been specially educated for that profession. But I am sure I shall like it much.'

'You have an opening?'

'I have not exactly got it, but I have advertised for one.'

'Lucy, you must let me help you!'

'Not at all.'

'You need not think it would compromise you, or that I am indifferent to delicacy. I bear in mind how we stand. It is very unlikely that you will succeed as teacher of the class you mention, so let me do something of a different kind for you. Say what you would like, and it shall be done.'

'No; if I can't be a drawing-mistress or governess, or

something of that sort, I shall go to India and join my brother.'

'I wish I could go abroad, anywhere, everywhere with you, Lucy, and leave this place and its associations for ever!'

She played with the end of her bonnet-string, and hastily turned aside. 'Don't ever touch upon that kind of topic again,' she said, with a quick severity not free from anger. 'It simply makes it impossible for me to see you, much less receive any guidance from you. No, thank you, Mr Barnet; you can do nothing for me at present; and as I suppose my uncertainty will end in my leaving for India, I fear you never will. If ever I think you *can* do anything, I will take the trouble to ask you. Till then, goodbye.'

The tone of her latter words was equivocal, and while he remained in doubt whether a gentle irony was or was not inwrought with their sound, she swept lightly round and left him alone. He saw her form get smaller and smaller along the damp belt of sea-sand between ebb and flood; and when she had vanished round the cliff into the harbour road, he himself followed in the same direction.

That her hopes from an advertisement should be the single thread which held Lucy Savile in England was too much for Barnet. On reaching the town he went straight to the residence of Downe, now a widower with four children. The young motherless brood had been sent to bed about a quarter of an hour earlier, and when Barnet entered he found Downe sitting alone. It was the same room as that from which the family had been looking out for Downe at the beginning of the year when Downe had slipped into the gutter and his wife had been so enviably tender towards him. The old neatness had gone from the house; articles lay in places which could show no reason for their presence, as if momentarily deposited there some months ago, and forgotten ever since; there were no flowers; things were jumbled together on the furniture which should have been in cupboards; and the place in general had that stagnant, unrenovated air which usually pervades the maimed home of the widower.

Downe soon renewed his customary full-worded lament over his wife, and even when he had worked himself up to tears, went on volubly, as if a listener were a luxury to be enjoyed whenever he could be caught.

'She was a treasure beyond compare, Mr Barnet! I shall never see such another. Nobody now to nurse me – nobody to console me in those daily troubles, you know, Barnet, which make consolation so necessary to a nature like mine. It would be unbecoming to repine, for her spirit's home was elsewhere – the tender light in her eyes always showed it; but it is a long dreary time that I have before me, and nobody else can ever fill the void left in my heart by her loss – nobody – nobody!' And Downe wiped his eyes again.

'She was a good woman in the highest sense,' gravely answered Barnet, who, though Downe's words drew genuine compassion from his heart, could not help feeling that a tender reticence would have been a finer tribute to Mrs Downe's really sterling virtues than such a second-class lament as this.

'I have something to show you,' Downe resumed, producing from a drawer a sheet of paper on which was an elaborate design for a canopied tomb. 'This has been sent me by the architect, but it is not exactly what I want.'

'You have got Jones to do it, I see, the man who is carrying out my house,' said Barnet, as he glanced at the signature to the drawing.

'Yes, but it is not quite what I want. I want something more striking – more like a tomb I have seen in St Paul's Cathedral. Nothing less will do justice to my feelings, and how far short of them that will fall!'

Barnet privately thought the design a sufficiently imposing one as it stood, even extravagantly ornate; but, feeling that he had no right to criticise, he said gently, 'Downe, should you not live more in your children's lives at the present time, and soften the sharpness of regret for your own past by thinking of their future?'

'Yes, yes; but what can I do more?' asked Downe, wrinkling his forehead hopelessly.

It was with anxious slowness that Barnet produced his reply – the secret object of his visit tonight. 'Did you not say one day that you ought by rights to get a governess for the children?'

Downe admitted that he had said so, but that he could not see his way to it. 'The kind of woman I should like to have,' he said, 'would be rather beyond my means. No; I think I shall send them to school in the town when they are old enough to go out alone.'

'Now, I know of something better than that. The late Lieutenant Savile's daughter, Lucy, wants to do something for herself in the way of teaching. She would be inexpensive, and would answer your purpose as well as anybody for six or twelve months. She would probably come daily if you were to ask her, and so your housekeeping arrangements would not be much affected.'

'I thought she had gone away,' said the solicitor, musing. 'Where does she live?"

Barnet told him, and added that if Downe should think of her as suitable, he would do well to call as soon as possible, or she might be on the wing. 'If you do see her,' he said, 'it would be advisable not to mention my name. She is rather stiff in her ideas of me, and it might prejudice her against a course if she knew that I recommended it.'

Downe promised to give the subject his consideration, and nothing more was said about it just then. But when Barnet rose to go, which was not till nearly bedtime, he reminded Downe of the suggestion and went up the street to his own solitary home with a sense of satisfaction at his promising diplomacy in a charitable cause.

CHAPTER SEVEN

The walls of his new house were carried up nearly to their full height. By a curious though not infrequent reaction, Barnet's feelings about that unnecessary structure had undergone a change; he took considerable interest in its progress as a long-neglected thing, his wife before her departure having grown quite weary of it as a hobby. Moreover, it was an excellent distraction for a man in the unhappy position of having to live in a provincial town with nothing to do. He was probably the first of his line who had ever passed a day without toil, and perhaps something like an inherited instinct disqualifies such men for a life of pleasant inaction, such as lies in the power of those whose leisure is not a personal accident, but a vast historical accretion which has become part of their natures.

Thus Barnet got into a way of spending many of his leisure hours on the site of the new building, and he might have been seen on most days at this time trying the temper of the mortar by punching the joints with his stick, looking at the grain of a floorboard, and meditating where it grew, or picturing under what circumstances the last fire would be kindled in the at-present sootless chimneys. One day when thus occupied he saw three children pass by in the company of a fair young woman, whose sudden appearance caused him to flush perceptibly.

'Ah, she is there,' he thought. 'That's a blessed thing.'

Casting an interested glance over the rising building and the busy workmen, Lucy Savile and the little Downes passed by; and after that time it became a regular, though almost unconscious custom of Barnet to stand in the half-completed house and look from the ungarnished windows at the governess as she tripped towards the seashore with her young charges, which she was in the habit of doing on most fine afternoons. It was on one of these occasions, when he had been loitering on the first-floor landing, near the hole left for the staircase, not yet erected, that there appeared above the edge of the floor a little hat, followed by a little head.

Barnet withdrew through a doorway, and the child came to the top of the ladder, stepping onto the floor and crying to her sisters and Miss Savile to follow. Another head rose above the floor, and another, and then Lucy herself came into view. The troop ran hither and thither through the empty, shaving-strewn rooms, and Barnet came forward.

Lucy uttered a small exclamation: she was very sorry that she had intruded; she had not the least idea that Mr Barnet was there: the children had come up, and she had followed.

Barnet replied that he was only too glad to see them there. 'And now, let me show you the rooms,' he said.

She passively assented, and he took her round. There was not much to show in such a bare skeleton of a house, but he made the most of it, and explained the different ornamental fittings that were soon to be fixed here and there. Lucy made but few remarks in reply, though she seemed pleased with her visit, and stole away down the ladder, followed by her companions.

After this the new residence became yet more of a hobby for Barnet. Downe's children did not forget their first visit, and when the windows were glazed, and the handsome staircase spread its broad low steps into the hall, they came again, prancing in unwearied succession through every room from ground floor to attics, while Lucy stood waiting for them at the door. Barnet, who rarely missed a day in coming to inspect progress, stepped out from the drawing-room.

'I could not keep them out,' she said, with an apologetic blush. 'I tried to do so very much: but they are rather wilful, and we are directed to walk this way for the sea air.'

'Do let them make the house their regular playground, and you yours,' said Barnet. 'There is no better place for children to romp and take their exercise in than an empty house, particularly in muddy or damp weather such as we shall get a good deal of now; and this place will not be furnished for a long, long time – perhaps never. I am not at all decided about it.'

'Oh, but it must!' replied Lucy, looking round at the hall. 'The rooms are excellent, twice as high as ours; and the views from the windows are so lovely.'

'I dare say, I dare say,' he said, absently.

'Will all the furniture be new?' she asked.

'All the furniture be new – that's a thing I have not thought of. In fact I only come here and look on. My father's house would have been large enough for me, but another person had a voice in the matter, and it was settled that we should build. However, the place grows upon me; its recent associations are cheerful, and I am getting to like it fast.'

A certain uneasiness in Lucy's manner showed that the conversation was taking too personal a turn for her.

'Still, as modern tastes develop, people require more room to gratify them in,' she said, withdrawing to call the children; and serenely bidding him good afternoon she went on her way.

Barnet's life at this period was singularly lonely, and yet he was happier than he could have expected. His wife's estrangement and absence, which promised to be permanent, left him free as a boy in his movements, and the solitary walks that he took gave him ample opportunity for chastened reflection on what might have been his lot if he had only shown wisdom enough to claim Lucy Savile when there was no bar between their lives, and she was to be had for the asking. He would occasionally call at the house of his friend Downe; but there was scarcely enough in common between their two natures to make them more than friends of that excellent sort whose personal knowledge of each other's history and character is always in excess of intimacy, whereby they are not so likely to be severed by a clash of sentiment as in cases where intimacy springs up in excess of knowledge. Lucy was never visible at these times, being either engaged in the schoolroom, or in taking an airing out of doors; but, knowing that she was now comfortable, and had given up the – to him – depressing idea of going off to the other side of the globe, he was quite content.

The new house had so far progressed that the gardeners were beginning to grass down the front. During an afternoon which he was passing in marking the curve for the carriage-drive, he beheld her coming in boldly towards him from the road. Hitherto Barnet had only caught her on the premises by stealth; and this advance seemed to show that at last her reserve had broken down.

A smile gained strength upon her face as she approached, and it was quite radiant when she came up, and said, without a trace of embarrassment, 'I find I owe you a hundred thanks – and it comes to me quite as a surprise! It was through your kindness that I was engaged by Mr Downe. Believe me, Mr Barnet, I did not know it until yesterday, or I should have thanked you long and long ago!'

'I had offended you – just a trifle – at the time, I think?' said Barnet, smiling, 'and it was best that you should not know.'

'Yes, yes,' she returned, hastily. 'Don't allude to that; it is past and over, and we will let it be. The house is finished almost, is it not? How beautiful it will look when the evergreens are grown! Do you call the style Palladian, Mr Barnet?'

'I – really don't quite know what it is. Yes, it must be Palladian, certainly. But I'll ask Jones, the architect, for, to tell the truth, I had not thought much about the style. I had nothing to do with choosing it, I am sorry to say.'

She would not let him harp on this gloomy refrain, and talked on bright matters till she said, producing a small roll of paper which he had noticed in her hand all the while, 'Mr Downe wished me to bring you this revised drawing of the late Mrs Downe's tomb which the architect has just sent him. He would like you to look it over.'

The children came up with their hoops, and she went off with them down the harbour road as usual. Barnet had been glad to get those words of thanks; he had been thinking for many months that he would like her to know of his share in finding her a home such as it was; and what he could not do for himself, Downe had now kindly done for him. He returned to his desolate house with a lighter tread; though in reason he hardly knew why his tread should be light.

On examining the drawing, Barnet found that, instead of the vast altar-tomb and canopy Downe had determined on at their last meeting, it was to be a more modest memorial even than had been suggested by the architect; a coped tomb of good solid construction, with no useless elaboration at all. Barnet was truly glad to see that Downe had come to reason of his own accord; and he returned the drawing with a note of approval.

He followed up the house work as before, and as he walked up and down the rooms, occasionally gazing from the windows over the bulging green hills and the quiet harbour that lay between them, he murmured words and fragments of words, which, if listened to, would have revealed all the secrets of his existence. Whatever his reason in going there, Lucy did not call again: the walk to the shore seemed to be abandoned; he must have thought it as well for both that it should be so, for he did not go anywhere out of his accustomed ways to endeavour to discover her.

CHAPTER EIGHT

The winter and the spring had passed, and the house was complete. It was a fine morning in the early part of June, and Barnet, though not in the habit of rising early, had taken a long walk before breakfast, returning by way of the new building. A sufficiently exciting cause of his restlessness today might have been the intelligence which had reached him the night before that Lucy Savile was going to India after all, and notwithstanding the representations of her friends that such a journey was inadvisable in many ways for an unpractised girl, unless some more definite advantage lay at the end of it than she could show to be the case. Barnet's walk up the slope to the building betrayed that he was in a dissatisfied mood. He hardly saw that the dewy time of day lent an unusual freshness to the bushes and trees which had so recently put on their summer habit of heavy leafage, and made his newly laid lawn look as well established as an old manorial meadow. The house had been so adroitly placed between six tall elms, which were growing on the site beforehand, that they seemed like real ancestral trees; and the rooks, young and old, cawed melodiously to their visitor.

The door was not locked, and he entered. No workmen appeared to be present, and he walked from sunny window to sunny window of the empty rooms with a sense of seclusion which might have been very pleasant but for the antecedent knowledge that his almost paternal care of Lucy Savile was to be thrown away by her wilfulness. Footsteps echoed through an adjoining room, and bending his eyes in that direction, he perceived Mr Jones, the architect. He had come to look over the building before giving the contractor his final certificate. They walked over the house together. Everything was finished except the papering: there were the latest improvements of the period in bell-hanging, ventilating, smoke-jacks, fire grates, and French windows. The business was soon ended, and Jones, having directed Barnet's attention to a roll of wallpaper patterns which lay on a bench for his choice, was leaving to keep another engagement when Barnet said, 'Is the tomb finished yet for Mrs Downe?'

'Well – yes, it is at last,' said the architect, coming back and speaking as if he were in a mood to make a confidence. 'I have had no end of trouble in the matter, and, to tell the truth, I am heartily glad it is over.'

Barnet expressed his surprise. 'I thought poor Downe had given up those extravagant notions of his? Then he has gone back to the altar and canopy after all? Well, he is to be excused, poor fellow!'

'Oh no – he has not at all gone back to them – quite the reverse,' Jones hastened to say. 'He has so reduced design after design that the whole thing has been nothing but wasted labour for me, till in the end it has become a common headstone which a mason put up in half a day.'

'A common headstone?' said Barnet.

'Yes. I held out for some time for the addition of a footstone at least. But he said oh no, he couldn't afford it.'

'Ah, well – his family is growing up, poor fellow, and his expenses are getting serious.'

'Yes, exactly,' said Jones, as if the subject were none of his. And again directing Barnet's attention to the wallpapers, the bustling architect left him to keep some other engagement.

'A common headstone,' murmured Barnet, left again to himself. He mused a minute or two, and next began looking over and selecting from the patterns; but had not long been engaged in the work when he heard another footstep on the gravel without, and somebody enter the open porch.

Barnet went to the door – it was his manservant in search of him.

'I have been trying for some time to find you, sir,' he said. 'This letter has come by the post, and it is marked immediate. And there's this one from Mr Downe who called just now wanting to see you.' He searched his pocket for the second.

Barnet took the first letter – it had a black border and bore the London postmark. It was not in his wife's handwriting, or in that of any person he knew; but conjecture soon ceased as he read the page, wherein he was briefly informed that Mrs Barnet had died suddenly on the previous day at the furnished villa she had occupied near London.

Barnet looked vaguely round the empty hall, at the blank walls, out of the doorway. Drawing a long palpitating breath, and with eyes downcast, he turned and climbed the stairs slowly, like a man who doubted their stability. The fact of his wife having, as it were, died once already, and lived on again, had entirely dislodged the possibility of her actual death from his conjecture. He went to the landing, leant over the balusters, and after a reverie of whose duration he had but the faintest notion, turned to the window and stretched his gaze to the cottage further down the road, which was visible from his landing, and from which Lucy still walked to the solicitor's house by a cross-path. The faint words that came from his moving lips were simply, 'At last!'

Then, almost involuntarily, Barnet fell down on his knees and murmured some incoherent words of thanksgiving. Surely his virtue in restoring his wife to life had been rewarded! But, as if the impulse struck uneasily on his conscience, he quickly rose, brushed the dust from his trousers and set himself to think of his next movements. He could not start for London for some hours, and as he had no preparations to make that could not be made in half an hour, he mechanically descended and resumed his occupation of turning over the wall-papers. They had all got brighter for him, those papers. It was all changed – who would sit in the rooms that they were to line? He went on to muse upon Lucy's conduct in so frequently coming to the house with the children; her occasional blush in speaking to him; her evident interest in him. What woman can in the long run avoid being interested in a man whom she knows to be devoted to her? If human solicitation could ever effect anything, there should be no going to India for Lucy now. All the papers previously chosen seemed wrong in their shades, and he began from the beginning to choose again.

While entering on the task he heard a forced 'Ahem!' from without the porch, evidently uttered to attract his attention, and footsteps again advancing to the door. His man, whom he had quite forgotten in his mental turmoil, was still waiting there.

'I beg your pardon, sir,' the man said from round the doorway; 'but here's the note from Mr Downe that you didn't take. He called just after you went out, and as he couldn't wait, he wrote this on your study table.'

He handed in the letter – no black-bordered one now, but a practical-looking note in the well-known writing of the solicitor.

Dear Barnet – it ran – *Perhaps you will be prepared for the information I am about to give – that Lucy Savile and myself are going to be married this morning. I have hitherto said nothing as to my intention to any of my friends, for reasons which I am sure you will fully appreciate. The crisis has been brought about by her expressing her intention to join her brother in India. I then discovered that I could not do without her.*

It is to be quite a private wedding, but it is my particular wish that you come down here quietly at ten and go to church with us; it will add greatly to the pleasure I shall experience in the ceremony, and, I believe, to Lucy's also. I have called on you very early to make the request, in the belief that I should find you at home; but you are beforehand with me in your early rising. – Yours sincerely,

– C. Downe

'Need I wait, sir?' said the servant, after a dead silence.

'That will do, William. No answer,' said Barnet, calmly.

When the man had gone Barnet reread the letter. Turning eventually to the wallpapers, which he had been at such pains to select, he deliberately tore them into halves and quarters, and threw them into the empty fireplace. Then he went out of the house, locked the door, and stood in the front awhile. Instead of returning into the town, he went down the harbour road and thoughtfully lingered about by the sea, near the spot where the body of Downe's late wife had been found and brought ashore.

Barnet was a man with a rich capacity for misery, and there is no doubt that he exercised it to its fullest extent now. The events that had, as it were, dashed themselves together into one half-hour of this day showed that curious refinement of cruelty in their arrangement which often proceeds from the bosom of the whimsical god at other times known as blind Circumstance. That his few minutes of hope, between the reading of the first and second letters, had carried him to extraordinary heights of rapture was proved by the immensity of his suffering now. The sun blazing into his face would have shown a close watcher that a horizontal line, which had never been seen before, but which was never to be gone thereafter, was somehow gradually forming itself in the smooth of his forehead. His eyes, of a light hazel, had a curious look which can only be described by the word bruised; the sorrow that looked from them being largely mixed with the surprise of a man taken unawares.

The secondary particulars of his present position, too, were odd enough, though for some time they appeared to engage little of his attention. Not a soul in the town knew, as yet, of his wife's death, and he almost owed Downe the kindness of not publishing it till the day was over: the conjuncture, taken with that which had accompanied the death of Mrs Downe, being so singular as to be quite sufficient to darken the pleasure of the impressionable solicitor to a cruel extent if made known to him. But as Barnet could not set out on his journey to London, where his wife lay, for some hours (there being at this date no railway within a distance of many miles), no great reason existed why he should leave the town.

Impulse in all its forms characterised Barnet, and when he heard the distant clock strike the hour of ten his feet began to carry him up the harbour road with the manner of a man who must do something to bring himself to life. He passed Lucy Savile's old house, his own new one, and came in view of the church. Now he gave a perceptible start, and his mechanical condition went away. Before the church gate were a couple of carriages, and Barnet then could perceive that the marriage between Downe and Lucy was at that moment being solemnised within. A feeling of sudden, proud self-confidence, an indocile wish to walk unmoved in spite of grim environments, plainly possessed him, and when he reached the wicket-gate he turned in without apparent effort. Pacing up the paved footway he entered the church, and stood for a while in the nave passage. A group of people was standing round the vestry door. Barnet advanced through these and stepped into the vestry.

There they were, busily signing their names. Seeing Downe about to look round, Barnet averted his somewhat disturbed face for a second or two; when he turned again front to front he was calm and quite smiling; it was a creditable triumph over himself, and deserved to be remembered in his native town. He greeted Downe heartily, offering his congratulations.

It seemed as if Barnet expected a half-guilty look upon Lucy's face; but no, save the natural flush and flurry engendered by the service just performed, there was nothing whatever in her bearing which showed a disturbed mind: her grey-brown eyes carried in them now as at other times the well-known expression of common-sensed rectitude which never went so far as to touch on hardness. She shook hands with him, and Downe said warmly, 'I wish you could have come sooner: I called on purpose to ask you. You'll drive back with us now?'

'No, no,' said Barnet. 'I am not at all prepared; but I thought I would look in upon you for a moment, even though I had not time to go home and dress. I'll stand back and see you pass out, and observe the effect of the spectacle upon myself as one of the public.'

Then Lucy and her husband laughed, and Barnet laughed and retired; and the quiet little party went gliding down the nave and towards the porch, Lucy's new silk dress sweeping with a smart rustle round the base-mouldings of the ancient font, and Downe's little daughters following in a state of round-eyed interest in their position, and that of Lucy, their teacher and friend.

So Downe was comforted after his Emily's death, which had taken place twelve months, two weeks, and three days before that time.

When the two flys had driven off and the spectators had vanished, Barnet followed to the door, and went out into the sun. He took no more trouble to preserve a spruce exterior; his step was unequal, hesitating, almost convulsive; and the slight changes of colour which went on in his face seemed refracted from some inward flame. In the churchyard he became pale as a summer cloud, and finding it not easy to proceed, he sat down on one of the tombstones and supported his head with his hand.

Hard by was a sexton filling up a grave which he had not found time to finish on the previous evening. Observing Barnet, he went up to him, and recognising him, said, 'Shall I help you home, sir?'

'Oh no, thank you,' said Barnet, rousing himself and standing up. The sexton returned to his grave, followed by Barnet, who, after watching him awhile, stepped into the grave, now nearly filled, and helped to tread in the earth.

The sexton apparently thought his conduct a little singular, but he made no observation, and when the grave was full, Barnet suddenly stopped, looked far away, and with a decided step proceeded to the gate and vanished. The sexton rested on his shovel and looked after him for a few moments, and then began banking up the mound.

In those short minutes of treading in the dead man Barnet had formed a design, but what it was the inhabitants of that town did not for some long time imagine. He went home, wrote several letters of business, called on his lawyer, an old man of the same place who had been the legal adviser of Barnet's father before him, and during the evening overhauled a large quantity of letters and other documents in his possession. By eleven o'clock the heap of papers in and before Barnet's grate had reached formidable dimensions, and he began to burn them. This, owing to their quantity, it was not so easy to do as he had expected, and he sat long into the night to complete the task.

The next morning Barnet departed for London, leaving a note for Downe to inform him of Mrs Barnet's sudden death, and that he was gone to bury her; but when a thrice-sufficient time for that purpose had elapsed, he was not seen again in his accustomed walks, or in his new house, or in his old one. He was gone for good, nobody knew whither. It was soon discovered that he had empowered his lawyer to dispose of all his property, real and personal, in the borough, and pay in the proceeds to the account of an unknown person at one of the large London banks. The person was by some supposed to be himself under an assumed name; but few, if any, had certain knowledge of that fact.

The elegant new residence was sold with the rest of his possessions, and its purchaser was no other than Downe, now a thriving man in the borough, and one whose growing family and new wife required more roomy accommodation than was afforded by the little house up the narrow side-street. Barnet's old habitation was bought by the trustees of the Congregational Baptist body in that town, who pulled down the time-honoured dwelling and built a new chapel on its site. By the time the last hour of that – to Barnet – eventful year had chimed, every vestige of him had disappeared from the precincts of his native place, and the name became extinct in the borough of Port Bredy, after having been a living force therein for more than two hundred years.

CHAPTER NINE

Twenty-one years and six months do not pass without setting a mark even upon durable stone and triple brass; upon humanity such a period works nothing less than transformation. In Barnet's old birthplace vivacious young children with bones like India rubber had grown up to be stable men and women; men and women had dried in the skin, stiffened, withered, and sunk into decrepitude; while selections from every class had been consigned to the outlying cemetery. Of inorganic differences the greatest was that a railway had invaded the town, tying it onto a main line at a junction a dozen miles off. Barnet's house on the harbour road, once so insistently new, had acquired a respectable mellowness, with ivy, Virginia creepers, lichens, damp patches, and even constitutional infirmities of its own like its elder fellows. Its architecture, once so very improved and modern, had already become stale in style, without having reached the dignity of being old-fashioned. Trees about the harbour road had increased in circumference or disappeared under the saw, while the church had had such a tremendous practical joke played upon it by some facetious restorer or other as to be scarce recognisable by its dearest old friends.

During this long interval George Barnet had never once been seen or heard of in the town of his fathers.

It was the evening of a market-day, and some half-dozen middle-aged farmers and dairymen were lounging round the bar of the Black Bull Hotel, occasionally dropping a remark to each other, and less frequently to the two barmaids who stood within the pewter-topped counter in a perfunctory attitude of attention, these latter sighing and making a private observation to one another at odd intervals, on more interesting experiences than the present.

'Days get shorter,' said one of the dairymen, as he looked towards the street, and noticed that the lamplighter was passing by.

The farmers merely acknowledged by their countenances the propriety of this remark, and finding that nobody else spoke, one of the barmaids said 'Yes', in a tone of painful duty.

'Come fair-day we shall have to light up before we start for home-along.'

'That's true,' his neighbour conceded, with a gaze of blankness.

'And after that we shan't see much further difference all's winter.'

The rest were not unwilling to go even so far as this.

The barmaid sighed again, and raised one of her hands from the counter on which they rested to scratch the smallest surface of her face with the smallest of her fingers. She looked towards the door, and presently remarked, 'I think I hear the bus coming in from station.'

The eyes of the dairymen and farmers turned to the glass door dividing the hall from the porch, and in a minute or two the omnibus drew up outside. Then there was a lumbering down of luggage, and then a man came into the hall, followed by a porter with a portmanteau on his poll, which he deposited on a bench.

The stranger was an elderly person, with curly ashen-white hair, a deeply creviced outer corner to each eyelid, and a countenance baked by innumerable suns to the colour of terracotta, its hue and that of his hair contrasting like heat and cold respectively. He walked meditatively and gently, like one who was fearful of disturbing his own mental equilibrium. But whatever lay at the bottom of his breast had evidently made him so accustomed to its situation there that it caused him little practical inconvenience.

He paused in silence while, with his dubious eyes fixed on the barmaids, he seemed to consider himself. In a moment or two he addressed them, and asked to be accommodated for the night. As he waited he looked curiously round the hall, but said nothing. As soon as invited he disappeared up the staircase, preceded by a chambermaid and candle, and followed by a lad with his trunk. Not a soul had recognised him.

A quarter of an hour later, when the farmers and dairymen had driven off to their homesteads in the country, he came downstairs, took a biscuit and one glass of wine, and walked out into the town, where the radiance from the shop windows had grown so in volume of late years as to flood with cheerfulness every standing cart, barrow, stall, and idler that occupied the wayside, whether shabby or genteel. His chief interest at present seemed to lie in the names painted over the shop-fronts and on doorways, as far as they were visible; these now differed to an ominous extent from what they had been one and twenty years before.

The traveller passed on till he came to the bookseller's, where he looked in through the glass door. A fresh-faced young man was standing behind the counter, otherwise the shop was empty. The grey-haired observer entered, asked for some periodical by way of paying for admission, and with his elbow on the counter began to turn over the pages he had bought, though that he read nothing was obvious.

At length he said, 'Is old Mr Watkins still alive?' in a voice which had a curious youthful cadence in it even now.

'My father is dead, sir,' said the young man.

'Ah, I am sorry to hear it,' said the stranger. 'But it is so many years since I last visited this town that I could hardly expect it should be otherwise.' After a short silence he continued: 'And is the firm of Barnet, Browse, and Company still in existence? – they used to be large flax-merchants and twine-spinners here?'

'The firm is still going on, sir, but they have dropped the name of Barnet. I believe that was a sort of fancy name – at least, I never knew of any living Barnet. 'Tis now Browse and Co.'

'And does Andrew Jones still keep on as architect?'

'He's dead, sir.'

'And the vicar of St Mary's – Mr Melrose?'

'He's been dead a great many years.'

'Dear me!' He paused yet longer, and cleared his voice. 'Is Mr Downe, the solicitor, still in practice?'

'No, sir, he's dead. He died about seven years ago.'

Here it was a longer silence still; and an attentive observer would have noticed that the paper in the stranger's hand increased its imperceptible tremor to a visible shake. That grey-haired gentleman noticed it himself, and rested the paper on the counter. 'Is *Mrs*

Downe still alive?' he asked, closing his lips firmly as soon as the words were out of his mouth, and dropping his eyes.

'Yes, sir, she's alive and well. She's living at the old place.'

'In East Street?'

'Oh no; at Château Ringdale. I believe it has been in the family for some generations.'

'She lives with her children, perhaps?'

'No; she has no children of her own. There were some Miss Downes – I think they were Mr Downe's daughters by a former wife – but they are married and living in other parts of the town. Mrs Downe lives alone.'

'Quite alone?'

'Yes, sir; quite alone.'

The newly arrived gentleman went back to the hotel and dined; after which he made some change in his dress, shaved back his beard to the fashion that had prevailed twenty years earlier, when he was young and interesting, and, once more emerging, bent his steps in the direction of the harbour road. Just before getting to the point where the pavement ceased and the houses isolated themselves, he overtook a shambling, stooping, unshaven man, who at first sight appeared like a professional tramp, his shoulders having a perceptible greasiness as they passed under the gaslight. Each pedestrian momentarily turned and regarded the other, and the tramp-like gentleman started back.

'Good – why – is that Mr Barnet? 'Tis Mr Barnet, surely!'

'Yes; and you are Charlson?'

'Yes – ah – you notice my appearance. The Fates have rather ill-used me. By the by, that fifty pounds. I never paid it, did I?... But I was not ungrateful!' Here the stooping man laid one hand emphatically on the palm of the other. 'I gave you a chance, Mr George Barnet, which many men would have thought full value received – the chance to marry your Lucy. As far as the world was concerned, your wife was a *drowned woman*, hey?'

'Heaven forbid all that, Charlson!'

'Well, well, 'twas a wrong way of showing gratitude, I suppose. And now a drop of something to drink for old acquaintance' sake! And Mr Barnet, she's again free – there's a chance now if you care for it – ha, ha!' And the speaker pushed his tongue into his hollow cheek and slanted his eye in the old fashion.

'I know all,' said Barnet, quickly; and slipping a small present into the hands of the needy, saddening man, he stepped ahead and was soon in the outskirts of the town.

He reached the harbour road, and paused before the entrance to a well-known house. It was so highly bosomed in trees and shrubs planted since the erection of the building that one would scarcely have recognised the spot as that which had been a mere neglected slope till chosen as a site for a dwelling. He opened the swing-gate, closed it noiselessly, and gently moved into the semicircular drive, which remained exactly as it had been marked out by Barnet on the morning when Lucy Savile ran in to thank him for procuring her the post of governess to Downe's children. But the growth of trees and bushes which revealed itself at every step was beyond all expectation; sun-proof and moon-proof bowers vaulted the walks, and the walls of the house were uniformly bearded with creeping plants as high as the first-floor windows.

After lingering for a few minutes in the dusk of the bending boughs, the visitor rang the doorbell, and on the servant appearing, he announced himself as 'an old friend of Mrs Downe's'.

The hall was lit, but not brightly, the gas being turned low, as if visitors were rare. There was a stagnation in the dwelling; it seemed to be waiting. Could it really be waiting for him? The partitions which had been probed by Barnet's walking-stick when the mortar was green, were now quite brown with the antiquity of their varnish, and the ornamental woodwork of the staircase, which had glistened with a pale yellow newness when first erected, was now of a rich wine-colour. During the servant's absence the following colloquy could be dimly heard through the nearly closed door of the drawing-room.

'He didn't give his name?'

'He only said "an old friend", ma'am.'

'What kind of gentleman is he?'

'A staidish gentleman, with grey hair.'

The voice of the second speaker seemed to affect the listener greatly. After a pause, the lady said, 'Very well, I will see him.'

And the stranger was shown in face to face with the Lucy who had once been Lucy Savile. The round cheek of that formerly young lady had, of course, alarmingly flattened its curve in her modern representative; a pervasive greyness overspread her once dark brown hair, like morning rime on heather. The parting down the middle was wide and jagged; once it had been a thin white line, a narrow crevice between two high banks of shade. But there was still enough left to form a handsome knob behind, and some curls beneath inwrought with a few hairs like silver wires were very becoming. In her eyes the only modification was that their originally mild rectitude of expression had become a little more stringent than heretofore. Yet she was still girlish – a girl who had been gratuitously weighted by destiny with a burden of five and forty years instead of her proper twenty.

'Lucy, don't you know me?' he said, when the servant had closed the door.

'I knew you the instant I saw you!' she returned, cheerfully. 'I don't know why, but I always thought you would come back to your old town again.'

She gave him her hand, and then they sat down. 'They said you were dead,' continued Lucy, 'but I never thought so. We should have heard of it for certain if you had been.'

'It is a very long time since we met.'

'Yes; what you must have seen, Mr Barnet, in all these roving years, in comparison with what I have seen in this quiet place!' Her face grew more serious. 'You know my husband has been dead a long time? I am a lonely old woman now, considering what I have been; though Mr Downe's daughters – all married – manage to keep me pretty cheerful.'

'And I am a lonely old man, and have been any time these twenty years.'

'But where have you kept yourself? And why did you go off so mysteriously?'

'Well, Lucy, I have kept myself a little in America, and a

little in Australia, a little in India, a little at the Cape, and so on; I have not stayed in any place for a long time, as it seems to me, and yet more than twenty years have flown. But when people get to my age two years go like one! – Your second question, why did I go away so mysteriously, is surely not necessary. You guessed why, didn't you?'

'No, I never once guessed,' she said, simply; 'nor did Charles, nor did anybody as far as I know.'

'Well, indeed! Now think it over again, and then look at me and say if you can't guess?'

She looked him in the face with an enquiring smile. 'Surely not because of me?' she said, pausing at the commencement of surprise.

Barnet nodded, and smiled again; but his smile was sadder than hers.

'Because I married Charles?' she asked.

'Yes; solely because you married him on the day I was free to ask you to marry me. My wife died four and twenty hours before you went to church with Downe. The fixing of my journey at that particular moment was because of her funeral; but once away I knew I should have no inducement to come back, and took my steps accordingly.'

Her face assumed an aspect of gentle reflection, and she looked up and down his form with great interest in her eyes. 'I never thought of it!' she said. 'I knew, of course, that you had once implied some warmth of feeling towards me, but I concluded that it passed off. And I have always been under the impression that your wife was alive at the time of my marriage. Was it not stupid of me! – But you will have some tea or something? I have never dined late, you know, since my husband's death. I have got into the way of making a regular meal of tea. You will have some tea with me, will you not?'

The travelled man assented quite readily, and tea was brought in. They sat and chatted over the tray, regardless of the flying hour. 'Well, well!' said Barnet, presently, as for the first time he leisurely surveyed the room. 'How like it all is, and yet how different! Just where your piano stands was a board on a couple of trestles, bearing the patterns of wallpapers when I was last here. I was choosing them – standing in this way, as it might be. Then my servant came in at the door, and handed me a note, so. It was from Downe, and announced that you were just going to be married to him. I chose no more wallpapers – tore up all those I had selected, and left the house. I never entered it again till now.'

'Ah, at last I understand it all,' she murmured.

They had both risen and gone to the fireplace. The mantel came almost on a level with her shoulder, which gently rested against it, and Barnet laid his hand upon the shelf close beside her shoulder. 'Lucy,' he said, 'better late than never. Will you marry me now?'

She started back, and the surprise which was so obvious in her wrought even greater surprise in him that it should be so. It was difficult to believe that she had been quite blind to the situation, and yet all reason and common sense went to prove that she was not acting.

'You take me quite unawares by such a question!' she said, with a forced laugh of uneasiness. It was the first time she had shown any embarrassment at all. 'Why,' she added, 'I couldn't marry you for the world.'

'Not after all this! Why not?'

'It is – I would – I really think I may say it – I would upon the whole rather marry you, Mr Barnet, than any other man I have ever met, if I ever dreamt of marriage again. But I don't dream of it – it is quite out of my thoughts; I have not the least intention of marrying again.'

'But – on my account – couldn't you alter your plans a little? Come!'

'Dear Mr Barnet,' she said, with a little flutter, 'I would on your account if on anybody's in existence. But you don't know in the least what it is you are asking – such an impracticable thing – I won't say ridiculous, of course, because I see that you are really in earnest, and earnestness is never ridiculous to my mind.'

'Well, yes,' said Barnet more slowly, dropping her hand, which he had taken at the moment of pleading, 'I am in earnest. The resolve, two months ago, at the Cape, to come back once more was, it is true, rather sudden, and as I see now, not well considered. But I am in earnest in asking.'

'And I in declining. With all good feeling and all kindness, let me say that I am quite opposed to the idea of marrying a second time.'

'Well, no harm has been done,' he answered, with the same subdued and tender humorousness that he had shown on such occasions in early life. 'If you really won't accept me, I must put up with it, I suppose.' His eye fell on the clock as he spoke. 'Had you any notion that it was so late?' he asked. 'How absorbed I have been!'

She accompanied him to the hall, helped him to put on his overcoat, and let him out of the house herself.

'Goodnight,' said Barnet, on the doorstep, as the lamp

shone in his face. 'You are not offended with me?'

'Certainly not. Nor you with me?'

'I'll consider whether I am or not,' he pleasantly replied. 'Goodnight.'

She watched him safely through the gate; and when his footsteps had died away upon the road, closed the door softly and returned to the room. Here the modest widow long pondered his speeches, with eyes dropped to an unusually low level. Barnet's urbanity under the blow of her refusal greatly impressed her. After having his long period of probation rendered useless by her decision, he had shown no anger, and had philosophically taken her words as if he deserved no better ones. It was very gentlemanly of him, certainly; it was more than gentlemanly: it was heroic and grand. The more she meditated, the more she questioned the virtue of her conduct in checking him so peremptorily, and went to her bedroom in a mood of dissatisfaction. On looking in the glass she was reminded that there was not so much remaining of her former beauty as to make his frank declaration an impulsive natural homage to her cheeks and eyes; it must undoubtedly have arisen from an old staunch feeling of his, deserving tenderest consideration. She recalled to her mind with much pleasure that he had told her he was staying at the Black Bull Hotel; so that if after waiting a day or two he should not, in his modesty, call again, she might then send him a nice little note. To alter her views for the present was far from her intention, but she would allow herself to be induced to reconsider the case, as any generous woman ought to do.

The morrow came and passed, and Mr Barnet did not

drop in. At every knock, light youthful hues flew across her cheek, and she was abstracted in the presence of her other visitors. In the evening she walked about the house, not knowing what to do with herself; the conditions of existence seemed totally different from those which ruled only four and twenty short hours ago. What had been at first a tantalising elusive sentiment was getting acclimatised within her as a definite hope, and her person was so informed by that emotion that she might almost have stood as its emblematical representative by the time the clock struck ten. In short, an interest in Barnet precisely resembling that of her early youth led her present heart to belie her yesterday's words to him, and she longed to see him again.

The next day she walked out early, thinking she might meet him in the street. The growing beauty of her romance absorbed her, and she went from the street to the fields, and from the fields to the shore, without any consciousness of distance, till reminded by her weariness that she could go no further. He had nowhere appeared. In the evening she took a step which under the circumstances seemed justifiable; she wrote a note to him at the hotel, inviting him to tea with her at six precisely, and signing her note 'Lucy'.

In a quarter of an hour the messenger came back. Mr Barnet had left the hotel early in the morning of the day before, but he had stated that he would probably return in the course of the week.

The note was sent back, to be given to him immediately on his arrival.

There was no sign from the inn that this desired event

71

had occurred, either on the next day or the day following. On both nights she had been restless, and had scarcely slept half an hour.

On the Saturday, putting off all diffidence, Lucy went herself to the Black Bull, and questioned the staff closely.

Mr Barnet had cursorily remarked when leaving that he might return on the Thursday or Friday, but they were directed not to reserve a room for him unless he should write.

He had left no address.

Lucy sorrowfully took back her note, went home, and resolved to wait.

She did wait – years and years – but Barnet never reappeared.

NOTES

1. Tophet refers to Topheth of the Old Testament – a place near Jerusalem where children were sacrificed to pagan gods. Tophet became another name for hell or a place of punishment.
2. Xanthippe was the wife of Socrates. History records her as being extremely bad tempered and the supreme example of the constantly nagging wife.
3. Hardy is here referring to the shipwreck of Aeneas at Carthage, as recounted in Virgil's *Aeneid*.

BIOGRAPHICAL NOTE

Thomas Hardy was born in Dorset in 1840, the son of a stonemason. From an early age he developed a love for music – his father in fact taught him the violin – and his mother instilled in him an interest in books and the countryside. A sickly child, Hardy did not attend school until the age of eight when he was sent to the county school in Dorchester. From there he was articled to a local architect, and then moved to London to work for Arthur Blomfield, the prominent architect. His continuing ill-health, however, forced him to return to Dorset.

In 1868 Hardy met Emma Gifford, who was later to become his wife. She encouraged him greatly in his writing, and his first published novel, *Desperate Remedies*, appeared in 1871. It met with very little success. However, *Under the Greenwood Tree*, published the following year, was widely read and brought Hardy popular acclaim. This early work, like much of his writing, incorporated many Dorset places into a fictional plot. *Under the Greenwood Tree* was followed by *A Pair of Blue Eyes* (1873), a serialised work, and *Far From the Madding Crowd* (1874) – the novel which finally allowed Hardy to leave architecture and begin to write full time.

Hardy and his wife moved around during the next few years, based mainly in Dorset but also living for a short while in London. They finally settled in Dorchester in 1887, in a house which Hardy himself had designed, and it was here that Hardy penned *The Mayor of Casterbridge* (1886), *The Woodlanders* (1887) and, perhaps his best-loved work, *Tess of the D'Urbervilles* (1891). *Tess* aroused considerable interest, but his next work, *Jude the Obscure* (1895), provoked a sea of controversy for its unorthodox treatment of marriage. Hardy was greatly surprised – and dismayed – by this reaction, and turned away from fiction, choosing instead to focus on poetry. He produced a number of volumes, including the famous *Wessex Poems* (1898).

Emma Hardy died in 1912, and Hardy was immediately stricken with grief and remorse. He poured out his feelings in his poetry, thereby producing some of the most moving lines he ever wrote. He was married again in 1914 – to Florence Dugdale, his secretary since 1912 – and the two of them remained in Dorchester until Hardy's death in 1928. He was buried in Poet's Corner in Westminster Abbey, although, in accordance with his wishes, his heart was placed alongside Emma's grave in Stinsford churchyard.

HESPERUS PRESS – 100 PAGES

Hesperus Press, as suggested by the Latin motto, is committed to bringing near what is far – far both in space and time. Works written by the greatest authors, and unjustly neglected or simply little known in the English-speaking world, are made accessible through new translations and a completely fresh editorial approach. Through these short classic works, each around 100 pages in length, the reader will be introduced to the greatest writers from all times and all cultures.

For more information on Hesperus Press, please visit our website: **www.hesperuspress.com**

ET REMOTISSIMA PROPE

SELECTED TITLES FROM HESPERUS PRESS

Gustave Flaubert *Memoirs of a Madman*

Alexander Pope *Scriblerus*

Ugo Foscolo *Last Letters of Jacopo Ortis*

Anton Chekhov *The Story of a Nobody*

Joseph von Eichendorff *Life of a Good-for-nothing*

Mark Twain *The Diary of Adam and Eve*

Giovanni Boccaccio *Life of Dante*

Victor Hugo *The Last Day of a Condemned Man*

Joseph Conrad *Heart of Darkness*

Edgar Allan Poe *Eureka*

Emile Zola *For a Night of Love*

Daniel Defoe *The King of Pirates*

Giacomo Leopardi *Thoughts*

Nikolai Gogol *The Squabble*

Franz Kafka *Metamorphosis*

Herman Melville *The Enchanted Isles*

Leonardo da Vinci *Prophecies*

Charles Baudelaire *On Wine and Hashish*

William Makepeace Thackeray *Rebecca and Rowena*

Wilkie Collins *Who Killed Zebedee?*

Théophile Gautier *The Jinx*

Charles Dickens *The Haunted House*

Luigi Pirandello *Loveless Love*

Fyodor Dostoevsky *Poor People*

E.T.A. Hoffmann *Mademoiselle de Scudéri*

Henry James *In the Cage*

Francis Petrarch *My Secret Book*

André Gide *Theseus*

D.H. Lawrence *The Fox*

Percy Bysshe Shelley *Zastrozzi*

Marquis de Sade *Incest*

Oscar Wilde *The Portrait of Mr W.H.*

Giacomo Casanova *The Duel*

Leo Tolstoy *Hadji Murat*

Friedrich von Schiller *The Ghost-seer*

Nathaniel Hawthorne *Rappaccini's Daughter*

Pietro Aretino *The School of Whoredom*

Honoré de Balzac *Colonel Chabert*

Arthur Conan Doyle *The Tragedy of the Korosko*

Stendhal *Memoirs of an Egotist*

Katherine Mansfield *In a German Pension*

Giovanni Verga *Life in the Country*

Ivan Turgenev *Faust*

Theodor Storm *The Lake of the Bees*

F. Scott Fitzgerald *The Rich Boy*

Dante Alighieri *New Life*

Guy de Maupassant *Butterball*

Charlotte Brontë *The Green Dwarf*

Elizabeth Gaskell *Lois the Witch*

Joris-Karl Huysmans *With the Flow*

George Eliot *Amos Barton*

Gabriele D'Annunzio *The Book of the Virgins*

Heinrich von Kleist *The Marquise of O–*

Alexander Pushkin *Dubrovsky*